Flora's Very Windy Day

by JEANNE BIRDSALL | illustrated by MATT PHELAN

sandpiper

HOUGHTON MIFFLIN HARCOURT

New York   Boston

www.hmhco.com

Hand-lettering by Leah Palmer Preiss. The illustrations were executed in ink, watercolors, and pastels.
The text was set in 14.5-point Horley Old Style MT Light. All rights reserved.

The Library of Congress has cataloged the hardcover edition as follows:
Birdsall, Jeanne.
Flora's very windy day/by Jeanne Birdsall; illustrated by Matt Phelan.
p. cm.
Summary: When a big wind blows her annoying little brother away, Flora decides to save him
despite the many tempting offers she gets for him from, among others, a cloud, an eagle,
the man in the moon, and the wind itself.
[1. Brothers and sisters—Fiction. 2. Wind—Fiction.] I. Phelan, Matt, ill. II. Title.
PZ7.B51197Fl 2010
[E]—dc22   2008056061

ISBN: 978-0-618-98676-7 hardcover
ISBN: 978-0-547-99485-7 paperback

Manufactured in China
SCP 10 9 8 7 6 5 4 3 2

4500513395

For Kelsey and Jesse—J.B.

For all the big sisters I know—M.P.

"Mommy! Crispin spilled my paints again!" shrieked Flora.

"I told you to keep your paints out of his reach," said her mother.

"I tried," said Flora, "but—"

"Oh, look at this mess. Outside, Flora. Right now!"

"I can't go outside," protested Flora. "The wind is very strong and will blow me away."

"Nonsense," said her mother.

Flora thought for a moment. "Of course, I could wear my super-special heavy-duty red boots. They'll keep me from being blown away."

"Fine," said her mother. "And take Crispin with you."

Now, Crispin did not have super-special heavy-duty red boots to protect him from the wind. His boots were purple and couldn't do anything but keep his feet dry.

Oh, well, Flora thought. It wouldn't be *her* fault if Crispin blew away.

So Flora put on her coat and hat
and her super-special heavy-duty red boots.

And her mother put Crispin
into his little coat and hat and regular
old purple boots.

And when all that was done,
Flora's mother opened the door and
Flora and Crispin stepped outside.

The wind was indeed very strong that day. It pushed and pulled, and twirled and twisted. But no matter how hard it blew, Flora stayed firmly on the ground.

"Ha ha! You dumb wind," said Flora. "You can't lift me up, because I'm wearing my super-special heavy-duty red boots!"

The wind did not like being laughed at. It doubled its strength and blasted mightily at Flora, but still she didn't budge.

"However," said Flora, "you may notice that my little brother is wearing regular old purple boots."

Now the wind tripled its strength. It swirled and swooped, and whizzed and walloped, and then—oh, my!—Crispin was being lifted off the ground.

Just a little bit at first, but the wind grew stronger and Crispin went higher, and then higher, and then higher still.

He was being blown away.

He looked very frightened.

And suddenly Flora was kicking off her super-special heavy-duty red boots and spreading her coat to the wind and—oh, my, oh, my!—she was sailing up toward Crispin.

She grabbed his hand and closed her eyes and
wished she were anywhere else in the world.

But soon Flora realized that being blown by the wind was comfortable, like riding along on a squishy flying chair. She decided to open her eyes.

Just then they came upon a dragonfly.
"Will you give me that little boy?" asked
the dragonfly. "He could polish my wings."

"Silly dragonfly," scolded Flora. She knew that
Crispin was too clumsy to clean such delicate wings.
"He's my brother and I'm taking him home."
"If the wind lets you," said the dragonfly.

Flora and Crispin flew on and on until they
came upon a sparrow.

"Will you give me that little boy?" asked the
sparrow. "He could sit on my eggs."

"What a mess that would be," said Flora. As if
Crispin could sit on eggs without breaking them.
"He's my brother and I'm taking him home."
"If the wind lets you," said the sparrow.

Flora and Crispin flew on and on until they came upon a rainbow.

"Will you give me that little boy?" asked the rainbow. "He could guard my pot of gold."

"Gold!" That was tempting. But, thought Flora,
Crispin's not fierce enough to guard anything. "No.
He's my brother and I'm taking him home."
"If the wind lets you," said the rainbow.

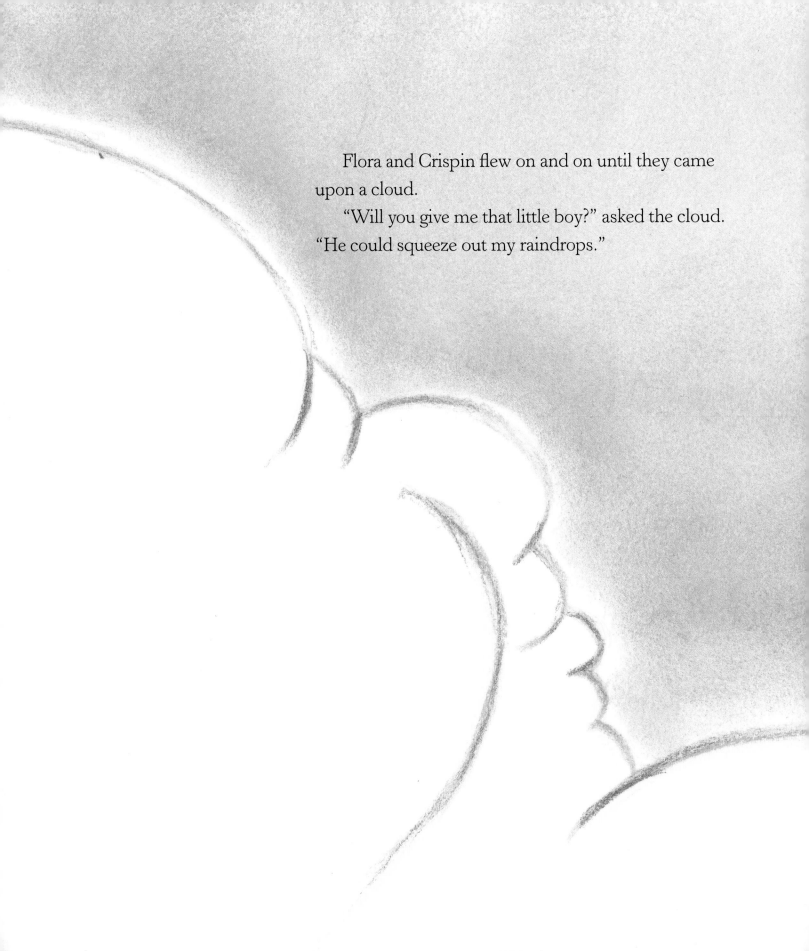

Flora and Crispin flew on and on until they came
upon a cloud.

"Will you give me that little boy?" asked the cloud.
"He could squeeze out my raindrops."

Flora thought that squeezing out raindrops sounded like fun.
But Crispin would surely catch a cold, and then who would help
him with his nose? "No, I won't give him to you. He's my brother
and I'm taking him home."

"If the wind lets you," said the cloud.

Flora and Crispin flew on and on until they came upon an eagle.
"Will you give me that little boy?" asked the eagle. "He could
sharpen my talons."

"You can't fool me," Flora said. She saw
the hungry look in the eagle's eye. "He's my
brother and I'm taking him home."

"If the wind lets you," said the eagle.

Flora and Crispin flew on and on until they came upon the man in the
moon.

"Will you give me that little boy?" asked the man in the moon. "It's lonely
up here, and he could keep me company."

The man in the moon had a kind face, and he did look awfully lonely. But
there were no chocolate chip cookies on the moon, and Crispin was so fond of
chocolate chip cookies. "I'm sorry, but I can't," said Flora. "He's my brother
and I'm taking him home."

"If the wind lets you," said the man in the moon.

Flora stomped her foot—or would have if there'd been anything
to stomp on. "I'm tired of hearing that. Why won't the wind let us go
home?"

"You should ask him," answered the man in the moon.

Flora hadn't thought of that. "Oh, wind, will you let us go home?"

"I'll let *you* go home as soon as we find the right spot for Crispin," replied the wind. "You do want to get rid of him, right?"

"Yes. I mean, I did. I mean—" Flora wasn't sure what she meant.

"Because I could even use him myself," said the wind. "You know, to work my bellows."

"No, thank you." Flora had finally decided. "I should
take him home. My mother wouldn't like it if I lost him."
"If that's what you really want," said the wind.
"Yes, please," said Flora.

So the wind turned Flora and Crispin around
and blew them home.

Flora put her super-special heavy-duty red boots
back on, then straightened Crispin's hat and brushed
a shred of rainbow from his coat.

She rang the doorbell and her mother opened the door.

"I decided to bring Crispin back," Flora told her.

"From where?" asked her mother.

"From the moon," said Flora.

"Nonsense," said her mother. "Now come inside. I've made chocolate chip cookies."